Walt Disney's RETURN TO OZ

Dorothy Returns to Oz

Based on the motion picture from Walt Disney Pictures
Directed by Walter Murch
Produced by Paul Maslansky
Executive Producer Gary Kurtz
Screenplay by Walter Murch and Gill Dennis

ISBN 0 361 06937 5
Copyright © 1985 Walt Disney Productions. All rights reserved.
Published 1985 by Purnell Books, Paulton, Bristol BS18 5LQ,
a member of the BPCC group.
Made and printed in Great Britain by
Purnell and Sons (Book Production) Limited, Paulton, Bristol

British Library Cataloguing in Publication Data
Dorothy returns to Oz.—(Adventure storybook
  series)
  I. Series
  823'.914[J]   PZ7
  ISBN 0-361-06937-5

Dorothy Gale's Aunt Em and Uncle Henry were worried.
Ever since the tornado, six months before, Dorothy had
been sad. She had been having bad dreams, and kept talking
about going back to her friends in a place she called Oz.

One morning when Dorothy was feeding the chickens, she found a strange key in the barnyard. She ran inside to show her aunt.

"Look, Aunt Em," she said. "It says 'OZ'. This proves Oz is real!"

Aunt Em shook her head sadly. "That's just the key to the old house," she said. Then she gave Dorothy a hug. "Uncle Henry and I have found a special doctor in Cottonwood Falls. He'll help you forget all about Oz so you can be happy again."

That afternoon Aunt Em took Dorothy over the river to
Dr. Worley's clinic in Cottonwood Falls.

Dr. Worley talked to Dorothy for a long time, and asked
her a lot of questions about Oz. Finally he said that Aunt Em
would have to leave her at the clinic for a while.

"Don't worry," he told Dorothy. "Nurse Wilson and I will
take care of you. You'll feel better in no time."

But Dorothy didn't feel better at the clinic. She felt sadder than ever. She missed Aunt Em, and Uncle Henry, and her dog Toto. One night there was a terrible storm. Dorothy sneaked out of her room, crept down the stairs, and ran out the door.

Outside, she ran to the river, which was churning wildly. Dorothy had no choice, she had to cross it. Closing her eyes and holding her breath, she jumped in.

As she struggled to stay afloat, a wooden chicken coop came drifting by. With a gasp of relief, Dorothy climbed into it, and in less than a minute, she was fast asleep.

When she woke up, the sun was shining and the water was calm. In fact, it was drying up! And something was clucking in the corner of the chicken coop.

"Billina!" Dorothy cried. Billina was her own favourite hen

from the barnyard at home. "What are you doing here?"

"This is a chicken coop, isn't it?" said Billina.

"You're talking," explained Dorohy. "Where did you learn to talk?"

"I'm not sure I know," said Billina. "Strange, isn't it?"

"It wouldn't be strange if this were Oz," said Dorothy, looking around. "And there's only one way to find out if it is. Let's go."

"If this is Oz," Dorothy explained, as she carried Billina through the woods, "we'll find the Yellow Brick Road, and that will lead us to the Emerald City. And in the Emerald City we'll find my friends—the Tin Woodman, the Cowardly Lion, and the Scarecrow. The Scarecrow is King of Oz now, you know. But before we find them, we have to find something to eat. I'm awfully hungry!"

They walked along, looking for fruit trees and berry
bushes. Suddenly Dorothy stopped. "Billina, look!"

In front of them was a tree with lunchpails
hanging from the branches.

"Oh, Billina, this *must* be Oz!" said Dorothy, plucking a
lunchpail from the tree.

"A perfect lunch," said Dorothy, as she and Billina
sat down to eat.

After lunch, Dorothy and Billina hurried on. Before long they came to a path that was strewn with stones and rubble—and broken yellow bricks.

"Oh, no," said Dorothy, her heart sinking. "Here's the Yellow Brick Road, but what's happened to it? Billina, we have to see if it still leads to the Emerald City."

But when they got to the Emerald City they found that it, too, was in ruins. And what was worse, everyone in it had been turned to stone—even the Tin Woodman and the Cowardly Lion.

"What's happened? Where is the Scarecrow?" Dorothy asked, growing more and more upset. "Where is—"

Her words were drowned out by a loud, horrible squealing.

Suddenly a mob of evil-looking, angry creatures, with wheels instead of arms and legs, surrounded the terrified Dorothy and Billina.

Taking Billina in her arms, Dorothy ran as fast as she could. The Wheelers rolled furiously after her.

With the Wheelers close behind, Dorothy darted down an alleyway. There was a wall at the end of it, with a door. If only she could get through that door . . .

All at once Dorothy remembered the key—the one she had found in the barnyard. She pulled it out of her pocket and tried it in the door.

It worked!

Dorothy and Billina found themselves in a small, dark room. Outside, the Wheelers squealed wildly and pounded on the door.

"What are we going to do now, Billina?" Dorothy asked. Then she saw something shining softly in the dim light.

It was a man, made completely of brass.

A sign on his chest said "Royal Army of Oz". Another sign, on his back, gave directions for winding up his speaking, thinking, and action works.

"I'll wind up his speaking first," said Dorothy. "Then he can tell us who he is."

"Good morn-ing," said the brass man. "I am Tik Tok,
the Roy-al Ar-my of Oz."

Dorothy introduced herself and Billina, and told Tik Tok
all that had happened. "Can you help us escape from the
Wheelers?" she asked as she wound up his action. "Can you
help us find the Scarecrow?"

Tik Tok gave a little bow. "From now un-til we find His
Ma-jes-ty the Scare-crow," he said, "I am your o-be-di-ent
ser-vant. Wind up my think-ing and I will form-u-late a
plan."

"Don't wor-ry a-bout the Whee-lers," Tik Tok continued. "I'll take care of them. Af-ter all, I'm the Roy-al Ar-my of Oz."

"Oh, Tik Tok," said Dorothy, carefully winding up his thinking, "I'm so glad we found you! Now that we're all together, I know we can find the Scarecrow. And when we do, everything will be all right again. After all—we're in Oz!"